About the Author

Simon has been chasing personal bests at Wycombe Rye parkrun since 2013 and has now completed 223 runs and 39 volunteer days. He had just completed his first time as run director and was about to do his second when lockdown kicked in. Simon retired from the corporate world in 2019 and now volunteers and works part-time for a local charity. This is Simon's first book which wouldn't exist if it weren't for lockdown. Some of the stories are semi-biographical, but most are drawn from the love of parkrun, the people and what it brings to people's lives.

Could Have Happened at parkrun

Simon C. Jones

Could Have Happened at parkrun

Olympia Publishers
London

www.olympiapublishers.com

OLYMPIA PAPERBACK EDITION

A CIP catalogue record for this title is
available from the British Library.

ISBN: 978-1-80074-113-3

This is a work of fiction.
Names, characters, places and incidents originate from the writer's
imagination. Any resemblance to actual persons, living or dead, is
purely coincidental.

First Published in 2021

Olympia Publishers
Tallis House
2 Tallis Street
London
EC4Y 0AB

Printed in Great Britain

Dedication

It's difficult to summarise how important the weekly parkrun has been to me since I started taking part in 2013. The stories in this book maybe a light-hearted look at certain behaviours and situations but I hope they convey the openness, honesty, community, and friendship that is embedded in parkrun. It is for that reason that this book is dedicated to my parkrun friends at Wycombe Rye, hoping we will be running together again soon. And Ray.

Acknowledgements

To Ruth, Becca and Cath, who support my eclectic interests. To the originators of parkrun, for the most wonderful event in the world. To Dad, who will treasure this, and Mum, who will never know.

parkrun lockdown stories

High Wycombe is a town in South Buckinghamshire, with beautiful parkland, minutes from the town centre. Fifty-three acres of land include a river, a waterfall, football fields, a boating lake, tennis courts, an open-air swimming pool, children's play areas, a café, a coffee kiosk, as well as numerous paths for walks both in the open and along tree-lined paths.

The Rye is also the location for the Wycombe Rye parkrun, which has taken place since August 2012 and now attracts between five hundred to six hundred runners every week, with another thirty people helping as volunteers. Wycombe Rye is an ideal course for a parkrun, providing an area for car parking right by the start and finish line, a café for drinks before and after the run and a swimming pool for cooling off after the event. There's a wide-open space for an easy start, an interesting mixture of paths and a return loop to the finish.

I have been running at Wycombe Rye parkrun since 2013. I started because I wanted to lose a bit of weight and keep fit but it has now become the essential start of my weekend. I look forward to meeting my friends in a friendly inclusive environment where the issues of the week are forgotten, and the only thoughts are of an improved pb and an enjoyable experience with others. Knowing that you are part of an event that is replicated all over the country, and many other places all over the world and supported by volunteers from every walk of life is a privilege that is hard to express.

My home parkrun at Wycombe Rye is probably like many others around. There are the unique features of the event, the unique characters that turn up and the unique situations that occur. I have tried to include some of these in my stories. The stories are all imaginary but use some of the experiences, some of the people and some of the situations that could relate to parkruns everywhere.

We are so fortunate to have parkrun. It's a place where people are happy, inclusive, supportive, friendly, welcoming, and eccentric. Some of the stories in this book were created as non-run reports as an escape for our time in lockdown, the rest are examples of my imagination running wild whilst we wait to get back together again.

I hope you enjoy them.

The parkrun stories

Run directors discuss the day's events

The run directors discuss their successful progress over the years and look back at the past with differing views of their experiences.

The volunteer coordinator

Helen, the volunteer coordinator, finds out that its easier than expected to sign up volunteers for next week's parkrun

Darren and his short Lead

Darren decides to take Marvin to parkrun, but his biggest challenge is buying a short lead.

The big thing in the city

Julian is desperate for people to appreciate his status away from parkrun but finds that his friends are just not interested.

Mr Shouty Man saves the day

Mr Shouty man fears his skills won't be needed until something unexpected happens to the PA system.

Edward Ready — 'Steady Eddy'

Steady Eddy has to get a PB every week, but when it starts to get more difficult, he decides to take matters into his own hands.

Martin, the funnel manager

Martin gets a bit of extra responsibility and finds out

that things aren't as complicated as he thought.

The visitor from New Zealand

A visitor from New Zealand gets lost in pronunciation.

Bobble and Trevor make friends

A new helper finds a friend, and everyone is calling his name.

Christopher, the competitive man in the queue

Christopher finds himself queuing in the wrong queue, and matters go from bad to worse in his attempt to beat his friend out of the car park

Petra and Jonathan manage the split

Petra and Jonathan find that their differing marshalling styles produce very different results.

A parkrun tourist come to Wycombe Rye

William wants to include Wigan in his parkrun poem but can't find anything to rhyme with it until he discovers High Wycombe

The run directors' discussion is an adaptation of the famous Four Yorkshiremen sketch from Monty Python. At the end of every run, the run directors get together and share a coffee whilst processing the result. I wondered what the conversation might have been when they realised that they had set a new record for the number of runners on a Saturday morning.

==

The Run directors' discussion. Overheard in the Lido, maybe…

NICK: Very successful, very successful indeed. Who'd have thought nearly eight years ago that we'd be sat here drinking espressos and cappuccinos, having processed and delivered the results to 666 parkrunners and 28 volunteers on our 384th parkrun?

ALISTAIR: Yes, in those days, we'd have been happy to have a hundred runners, and it would have taken most of the day to process the results.

CAROLYN: I remember a time before parkrun when we'd be glad to just have a run around the Rye.

NICK: Yes, a wet Rye!

ALISTAIR: Without marshals or bibs.

LYNDSAY: Or cones!

NICK: With a single stopwatch…

ALISTAIR: We never had a stopwatch! We used to count them all out, then count them all back.

CAROLYN: The best we could do was to hope the last one came back…

NICK: But we were happy in those days, even though there were only a few of us.

ALISTAIR: It's *because* there were only a few of us!

My old dad used to say to me, "Running on your own won't make you happy, son." And he was right, you have to run with someone!

I used to run around for hours looking for someone else to run with. I'd get up early and go out searching wearing an old pair of running shoes.

CAROLYN: You were lucky to have running shoes! I had to use my old plimsolls. I'd run round the Rye, slipping and sliding, with no idea of where to start or where to stop; there'd be no marshals, no cones, no bar codes or time stamps and only one piece of cake!

LYNDSAY: Ohhh, we used to dream of having a piece of cake; it would have been heaven for us. We used to huddle under a tree at the end, trying to share a biscuit.

ALISTAIR: Chocolate biscuit?

LYNDSAY: Yes.

ALISTAIR: You were lucky! We had no biscuits, and sometimes there were only six of us. By the time we'd sorted out someone to be the run director, time-keeper, the barcode scanner, volunteer coordinator and a couple of marshals, there was no one left to have a run!

CAROLYN: Two marshals?

ALISTAIR: Yes.

CAROLYN: You were lucky! We only had one marshal, and she had to cover all locations when the runners ran around. She'd set up all the cones, do the briefing, start the run, run across to the play area, then run to the boating lake, then run along the Dyke to the waterfall, then across to the steps, then back to the finish. By the time she'd finished, she was too tired to process the results.

LYNDSAY: We hardly ever processed our results; we were usually fighting over the biscuit.

NICK: Right... well, we had it tough. Firstly, there were no biscuits, cakes, or cones!

I used to get up in the morning at three a.m. at night and drive two hundred and fifty miles hoping that someone else would join us in the right place, at the right time. We had no start line, no finishing line, no briefing, no free t-shirts, marshals, cake or biscuits. We had no equipment, no internet, no run directors, no volunteers, no support from parkrun HQ or the local council and no community spirit. And, at the end of the day, no timed 5k run for anyone for free forever.

ALISTAIR: And you try to tell that to people who don't come to parkrun... and they won't believe you.

ALL: Nope!

The volunteer coordinator is quite an important role at parkrun, and I wondered what it would be like if the person who was given the role took it a bit too competitively and felt that the challenge was something more difficult than he or she eventually found.

==

The Volunteer Coordinator

It's 8.25 a.m. She arrives to take up her position. All week she's been thinking of this task. She is a mild-mannered person, always ready to smile, always welcoming and always friendly. Her day-to-day role is a piffling inconvenience compared to the challenge she's been asked to complete in these next ninety minutes. No one knows or understands the preparation she's gone through and the training she's endured to rise to the occasion, to compete on this day, and at this time, no one knows until the megaphone announces that today, Helen Philips is this week's Wycombe Rye parkrun volunteer coordinator.

Six hundred eyes turn to the desk where she is seated. She looks around, making as much eye contact with her prey as she can. *They'll be back,* she thinks to herself… *they have to be,* she smiles.

The runners look to see where Helen is seated.

They look at her volunteer list, and they look at her pen, they look at her… some make eye contact; they are doomed, she thinks… she'll remember them. As the runners depart to the start line, Helen looks at her sheet. Plenty of spaces to fill, she smiles. Plenty of runners to catch… she smiles again.

She looks at some of the names on the list; many have been caught before she thinks. Some regulars as well, even more interesting, she thinks.

She hears the runners start the run… not long now. In eighteen minutes, her destiny awaits, they'll be queuing up, and she has to get them to sign up; she just has to. Maybe she can pick them off one by one… she's feeling confident.

She looks around the table, all the enticements are there, cake, sweets, biscuits, and those little bits of flapjack that they sell in plastic containers from M&S… but will it be enough, she wonders?

She hears someone announce that the runners are returning, not long now. She makes herself comfortable in the chair; she doesn't want to look too relaxed; they might not take her seriously.

The first runner crosses the line; it's a fast one. *A long time to the second and third, nice,* she thinks to herself, *I'll have him all to myself for a bit longer.*

He gets scanned, approaches the board and carefully places his time token on the nail. He's relaxed, the time was OK but nothing special. As he thinks about the chances of a PB on the next occasion, Helen pounces. "Would you like to volunteer?" she says.

"I'd love to pet," he says, "but I'm a visitor from Bury St Edmunds, and I won't be back for a year."

Helen looks at her sheet as she starts to say, "That's no probl…" when she suddenly stops. The volunteer list only extends for three months.

She looks at the runner like a teacher looking at a pupil who has an excuse for not handing in his homework that is just about believable.

"OK," she finally says, "maybe next year then." She speaks slowly and deliberately. She looks at the finish line… plenty more to work on.

The next runner comes over; Helen checks the cakes.

"Good run?" she says, with a smile.

"Excellent," he says.

"Would you like to volunteer?" she says, her eyes glancing towards the cakes.

"Actually, I'm down to be marshal next week already."

Her eyes move back to the volunteer list. "Oh, I see," she says; the cakes are of no use now.

But she feels as though it's just worth checking.

"There I am," he says, pointing at the time-keeper role.

She squints and nods. "Ah, yes, OK then," she says. *At least he's on the list,* she thinks to herself.

The third person arrives; she places her token on the board and turns to look at the cake.

Not so fast lady, Helen thinks to herself…

"Would you like some cake?" she says, the hint in her voice just suggesting that it might be dependent on a bit of enthusiasm for a role on her list.

"Actually, I'm just checking the cake with the 250 on it. It's my 250th parkrun today, and I'm down to be a marshal next week. I try and do two runs followed by one volunteer week, so I should appear on the list a few times.

Helen is wide-eyed, not only at the size of the cake but at the thought of a runner with 250 runs and a least 125 volunteer points to her name.

"Wow," she says, desperately trying to add up 250 and 125 in her head.

"That's two hun… three hundr… over 400 times you attended parkrun?"

Maths wasn't her forte.

The fourth runner turns up.

Helen checks her list again; the cakes are ready. The flapjack carton is open. Here goes, but before she can speak…

"Hello," says the runner, "can I put my name down for a role next week?"

Helen is stunned. Her composure is blown. She's staring at the volunteer and the sheet, like someone being given too much cake to eat.

Another volunteer leans over the fourth one and starts pointing at roles they'd like to do.

"Can I be a scanner? I do like being the scanner or the funnel manager; that's a good one, running up and down shouting at people."

Someone else joins in, "How about the marshal at the split? That's a good one; you can see people going out and coming back."

They stop for a second to think.

"Actually, all the marshal roles get to see people going out and back. Put me down for a marshal role, please."

Two more people approach the desk. One says, "I'd like to volunteer for the time-keeper or that person that helps the token hander-outer please, and my friend would like to be the scanner person or the person with the clipboard who stands behind the scanner… please."

"No problem," says Helen, feeling a bit flummoxed. She wasn't expecting this.

For the next ten minutes, Helen fills up the list with a continuous flow of people. She's overwhelmed.

Helen spots a little girl standing with her mum near the runners queuing to place their tokens. The mum approaches Helen and asks if there's a role that her daughter can do to help her Duke of Edinburgh award.

"She's a bit shy but would really like to get involved," the mum says.

Helen thinks for a second and then suggests something. "There's a really good role for a nice person like your daughter..." she pauses, "it's the volunteer coordinator role, would that be, OK?"

Running with your dog is very popular at parkrun, but there are strict rules that all dogs must be on a short lead. I wondered what it would be like for a runner who wanted to run with his dog for the first time but had to go to buy a short lead first.

===

Darren and his short lead

"Why don't you take Marvin with you next time?" said Darren's wife, "he'd love the exercise, and you wouldn't have to do a parkrun then go for a five-mile walk straight afterwards."

He knew it made sense; it was tiring going for a long walk straight after doing parkrun; but Darren loved to compete for his personal bests and chat with all his parkrun friends on his own on a Saturday morning rather than have to look after their shaggy cockapoo, Marvin.

He thought about it as he got to the end of the walk and decided that maybe he should give it a try, just once. Maybe his wife wouldn't say the same thing every time he got back from the run if he tried it just once.

He arrived back home and walked into the kitchen.

"Right then," he announced, "starting next week, I will be running parkrun with Marvin."

Marvin looked at Darren, raised his ears and cocked his head to one side.

"All right, boy?" he looked at Marvin enthusiastically.

"That's a good idea," said his wife, "all you need to do now is get a new lead."

"What? But we've got a lead."

"You're not using that old lead to go running with, it's too long, and it will get wrapped around everyone's legs. You'll have to go down to Pets R Us and get one; according to parkrun, you just need to get a short one."

Darren hadn't wanted to go shopping for leads but organised to go the following day.

He walked into Pets R Us.

"I'd like a new dog lead, please," he said to the assistant.

"Certainly, sir, you've come to the right place, now what sort do you want? we have the standard flat lead, the bungee and stretchable rubber lead, the gentle leader headcollar, the harness lead, various slip leads, Martingale leads and retractable leads, unless, of course, you want to go running?"

"That's right, I need a short lead for my dog Marvin; we'll be running at parkrun."

"Oh dear," said the assistant, "oh dear, oh dear."

"What's up?" asked Darren.

"I'm afraid none of the leads I've mentioned is suitable if you want to go running at parkrun, sir; you need to select from our range of running leads, including…" he took a deep breath, "hands-free dog leads for puppies, hands-free leads for running, walking and hiking, a roadrunner quick release with LED attachment, A Premium running lead with an adjustable D Ring, a weather-resistant belt lead with a built-in shock absorber or with built-in reflective stitching."

"Well…" began Darren, assuming that he'd finished.

"One or two-handed leads for the use of either hand

or both, leads with built-in pooper scoopers, built-in bag holders and built-in pooper bags which can be empty or full. And we also have leads with built-in pockets for treats for the dog, and built-in bottles for water, for you or the dog, or you could share. But I should tell you, sir, that if you go for a lead with all the built-in options, they do tend to sag, especially on long runs."

"Well…" said Darren again, pausing to check that the assistant had finished. "I can see that this isn't going to be a quick decision."

The assistant raised his eyebrows, and his eyes widened. "Certainly not, sir, and we haven't even discussed the fitting session yet."

"Fitting session? said Darren.

"Oh yes, sir, firstly for you, then for your dog. I'm pleased to say that the days of coming to Pets R Us and asking for a short running lead are long gone, particularly since the case of the Dangling Dachshund."

"The Dangling Dachshund?" echoed Darren.

"You haven't heard of the Dangling Dachshund, sir? It was in all the pet trade magazines. A very tall runner came into one of our stores and asked for a short lead… I'm afraid the story is too difficult for some of us to recall without getting very emotional."

"I'm sorry to hear that," said Darren sympathetically.

"Thank you, sir, that's very kind of you. That's the reason why people like me are put in these positions of responsibility so that owners like yourself are not sold just any old short lead but a lead that is appropriate for your requirements and suitable for both you and your dog. It's why people like…" he stopped talking and rolled his eyes in the direction of another assistant in the store who was filling the shelves with tins of dog food then continued, "…are filling shelves with tins of dog food because they'd rather joke about these things than feel compassion for the poor doggie."

He calmed himself and took a deep breath.

"So, sir, shall we talk about the fitting session and the pre-fitting questionnaire?"

"Pre-fitting questionnaire?" Darren asked.

"Oh yes, sir, we have a special one for the parkrunners, it just makes sure we have all the issues covered, then, once that's done, we can arrange for the fitting session, you know, things like how tall you are, how long your arms are, stride length for you and the dog, how tall the dog is, etc., etc."

The assistant paused for a second.

"But I'm afraid we will need to know some other personal things about you, sir." The assistant looked very embarrassed and sheepish as he leant forward and spoke in a whisper.

Darren leant forward over the desk. Their heads were inches apart. The assistant looked around the store and got closer to Darren. He spoke very quietly and slowly.

"I'm afraid we'll need to know your PB and whether you think it's going to get better." His eyes widened again. "Or… worse."

"What!?" Darren was horrified. "Look, I'm sorry, but I didn't think this was going to get so personal," said Darren, who was now several shades redder than a sunburned Scotsman on his first holiday to Spain, ever!

"I'm so sorry, sir, but it's for the best; think of

Marvin, sir."

"But telling you whether my PB might get worse. I mean, there are some things *no one* admits to in public, and there are some things that are only discussed with your parkrun running pals, not just any Pets R Us—"

"Certified!" interrupted the assistant.

"What?" said Darren.

"Yes, sir, part of the parkrun questionnaire declaration is a sworn statement never to divulge the potential future parkrun PB, especially if it's likely to get slower, which means we're certified by Pets R Us."

"If anyone were to find out your future PB, I'd be stacking tins for the rest of my life… just like Kevin over there."

"Well, OK, but I'd like a fellow parkrunner to do the questionnaire."

"That's no problem at all, sir. We can certainly arrange to have a fellow parkrunner who is sworn to secrecy to do the questionnaire with you. Would that, be OK?"

"Well, OK, that might be acceptable," said Darren.

Darren stood back from the sales desk; his morning had been a lot more stressful than he'd anticipated. He took a deep breath; he never knew buying a lead would be so challenging.

He looked at the assistant, who in his turn could see that Darren was concerned.

He leant forward again. "You know, sir, there might be a way that we might be able to… you know, make sure that the future PB is, shall we say… faster."

Darren frowned, "You mean falsify the

questionnaire?" The sheer thought of it sent a shudder down his spine.

"I really couldn't imagine—" he started to say.

"Oh *no*, sir, I wouldn't dream of suggesting anything like that!" the assistant said hurriedly.

Darren relaxed; the prospect of getting involved in some serious skulduggery had been avoided.

"But we do have some, how do I say it, more serious leads for the more professional parkrunner who wants to improve their PB, with their canine companion."

Darren was intrigued, and the assistant could see that he was hooked. He opened a drawer under the counter and took out a box.

"What we have here, sir, is the very latest in lightweight, aerodynamic, low friction, aerospace-grade running leads that are almost guaranteed to improve a PB. This is called the 'K9 Whip-it' sir, very exclusive," he whispered, giving Darren a slight wink as he pointed to a specific lead in his drawer.

"You do understand that I can't guarantee that your PB will be faster, but I can certainly certify that it *might* be faster on the questionnaire…"

The intricacies of what the assistant was saying were sinking in…

"I see…" said Darren, mulling the situation over in his mind.

One fitting session later, one completed questionnaire safely filed, and the transaction was concluded. Darren walked out of Pets R Us with a spring in his step, a smile on his face, and a brand-new short lead.

The following Saturday, Darren arrived at parkrun with Marvin on his new lead. It didn't take long for Marvin to search out the other dogs who were there.

Darren looked at the lead of the other dog and then looked at the owner. The owner looked at Darren.

"Ah, the K9 Whip-it from Pets R Us?" said Darren, eyeing up the lead. He leaned forward and asked *sotto voce*, "Did you have to sign the questionnaire about, you know... the PB?"

"I did," said the other owner, looking a bit embarrassed, "I saw a very nice chap called Kevin."

Attending parkrun is a great leveller. Apart from the quality of a person's running shoes and the colour and number on a runner's back, there is no social hierarchy or status; everyone is just a runner. I wondered what it would be like for someone desperate to share his non-parkrun status with his parkrun friends, especially if they weren't that interested.

===

The big thing in the city

"But I know you're a really big thing in the city, dear," said Julian's wife, Sophie as he discussed his latest trip to Wycombe Rye parkrun.

"And plenty of your friends and colleagues know you're a really big thing in the city too."

"I know, but they only know me as Julian, the runner at parkrun and not the really big thing in the city that I know I am, and I can't go around shouting about it, can I?" said Julian.

"How about you turn up in the Mustang one day and let them see that? Then they might ask something," Sophie said, helpfully.

"Tried that," said Julian, "but the loud exhaust just set off a load of car alarms, and I didn't want to admit it was me,"

"Well…" she thought for a second. "How about wearing those really expensive Nike running shoes one day?"

"What, the really expensive ones?

"No silly… the really, *really* expensive ones that you got in America."

"Oh, *those* ones. No, I tried that, but everyone just said I'd better try and avoid the mud and, I don't think they realised just how really, really expensive they were. They just thought that they were new. I'm sure some people thought that I'd just washed them, and they weren't new or expensive at all!"

"Oh, dear," said his wife…

There was a long silence.

"How about…" she paused… "how about wearing that running watch that you've got, the one that tells you everything about your running and synchronises with your phone and everything?"

"Nah, they all have those down there."

"What about…" she paused again to think for a second. "What about going down in my Bentley and I drive, and I wear that new coat and have my hair done? Then someone's bound to ask if you're someone big, and I can just slip in that you're a really big thing in the city."

Julian thought about it for a second, "Um, I supposed I could say that the Aston was in the garage and that you had to drive me down…" he thought a bit longer.

"OK, let's try it next week."

The following weekend Julian and Sophie travelled down to parkrun in Sophie's Bentley. The roof was up because she didn't want the wind blowing her hair around. They got out, and Julian went to get a ticket for the car.

One of his running friends ran past back to his car. "Morning, Julian, I see you've got the chauffeur to bring you down this morning... looking forward to a good run?

"Yes, certainly am, the Aston's in the gar—" he started, but his friend was too far away to hear anyway.

He got his ticket and went back to the car.

"Right then," he said to Sophie, "Let's just walk in and act normally. By the way, you might want to stand on the steps by the Lido; there's quite a bit of mud where we meet up."

"Mud, you might have warned me before I wore my Jimmy's!"

Julian looked down at Sophie's new Jimmy Choo shoes.

"Oh, and they probably won't notice them anyway," he sighed.

They walked from the car park into the meeting area where all the parkrunners gathered to get ready for the run. The gazebo had just been put up, and the sheet was on the ground for the runners to place their bags and tracksuits.

"Morning, guys," said Julian to a bunch of his running friends.

"Morning," they all responded.

"Can I introduce my wife, Sophie? She had to bring me down this morning in the Bentley because the Aston's in the gar—"

"Morning, Sophie," they all responded.

"Come to see him get a new PB, have you? He's been on a bit of a roll recently, haven't you Julian? What was it last week, 23.55 and 24.02 the week before, pretty good going?"

"So, Sophie, are you checking out parkrun for a run in the future, or maybe running today? You can put the coat down there if you like?"

She looked down at the plastic sheet with tracksuits and sweatshirts piled high; the thought of placing her Loro Piana Cashmere coat on the pile sent a shudder down her back that made her shiver.

"Oh no, not running, just dropping Julian off because the Astons in the gar—"

"You know what, Sophie," said one of the runners interrupting Sophie in mid-sentence, "I think your Julian should take a break from trying for another PB today and have a go at being the pacer. They are short of a runner for thirty minutes, and that would be an ideal pace for Julian. What do you say, Julian? Sophie, can you convince him?"

They all looked at Sophie.

"Well..." she stuttered... she hadn't got a clue what they were talking about, so she just shrugged and smiled.

"There you go, Julian, Sophie agrees; I'll go tell the run director and get the bib."

"Bib?" said Sophie.

"Oh, it's just a yellow running bib to show you're the pacer," said one of the runners.

"Oh," said Sophie.

The run director pulled Julian to one side and briefed him on being the pacer.

"So, Sophie, has Julian had a good week. Do you think he's up to it?" asked one of the runners.

Sophie beamed; she took a deep breath. This was her chance to tell them that he was a really big thing in the city.

"Well, he has had a very busy week, actually. First, there was the trip to the States, then back to London for some big meetings, then Brussels on Friday morning and back late last night. It's been a very busy week; did you know that he's a really big—"

"Yes, but did he get any running in?"

"What? I mean pardon?" said Sophie, having been stopped at the crucial moment.

"Did he do any training in the week?"

"Training? Oh, *running*, you mean?"

"Well, yes…" said the parkrunner, confused by the question. "Did he manage to get out during the week and have a run?"

"Er, I think so," ventured Sophie.

"Ah, that's OK then, it's good to get out a least once a week. He's been running so well these last few weeks, and we're really pleased he's got so many PBs recently. I'm struggling a bit at the moment, and the others are way off their times. He gives us a lot to talk about when we meet up. He's a really good member of our group."

The run director gave the briefing and made the special mention that Julian would be doing the thirty-minute pace and that they should look out for him at the start. Julian waved his arm in the air and everyone gave him a clap and a cheer.

On the walk over to the start line, everyone asked Julian if he was OK about being the pacer and checking he had a watch and reminding him to hit each kilometre mark at six minutes.

"As long as you hit the markers at 6, 12, 18, 24 and finally 30 minutes, everything will be fine," said one of the regulars who was known to be pretty good at stating the obvious.

Julian looked back over his shoulder at Sophie, who was standing on the steps of the Lido trying to get the mud off her shoes and kicking herself for not having made better use of her chances to remind everyone that Julian was a really big thing in the city, but at the same time thinking about what the runner had told her about Julian.

They set off, and Julian got into a steady pace. It was quite comfortable for him to run at a slower pace, and he waved at Sophie as the runners ran past the Lido.

After the first kilometre, he could sense that there were quite a few runners who were running around him; some were struggling to keep up. He started to give them some encouragement.

"Well done, that's really good running!" he called out.

The runners who were trying to keep up with him looked up and tried to force a smile.

One of the runners beside him started talking to Julian.

"You must have been doing parkrun for quite a while; you're a really strong runner."

"Well, I try, it's difficult to get out as much as I'd like, but when I can, I like to try and challenge that PB, it's tricky because you see I'm a really big…" but the runner couldn't keep up and started dropping back.

Another runner came up beside him, and Julian could see they were struggling.

"Not long now, you're doing really well!" he shouted.

"Thanks," panted the runner…

"I was just telling the other runner that I'm a really big…"

"How much further?" gasped the other runner.

Julian stopped his original comments.

"Well, we're past the steps, so we must be more than halfway round. Keep it up; I'm sure you'll make it."

He started to drop back to the other runner, who was struggling.

"Keep it up; pretty soon, it'll be downhill all the way".

The runner tried to smile but was still battling.

"Just try and stick with me, one step at a time," said Julian, shouting encouragement.

Julian could see that there were about ten other runners all trying to keep up with him in addition to the struggling runner.

The last two kilometres were hard work; for Julian and the runners he was shouting encouragement to.

As they came round the last bend, fifteen people sprinted to the finish and got there ahead of Julian, who came in at exactly thirty minutes.

In the finish funnel, everyone around him thanked him for helping them get a new PB, and some of them were telling the run director how good Julian was.

The run director had the microphone in his hand and lifted it to his mouth.

"Let's have a big shout out for our pace runner Julian this morning; not only did he come in at thirty minutes, but he got fifteen runners round with new PB, and that's a really big thing!"

Many runners gave out a big cheer, except most of the runners in the funnel who were too tired to say anything.

Julian looked over to Sophie and smiled.

In the car on the way home, they were quiet, lost in their thoughts. Julian was the first to speak.

"So, maybe you don't need to drive me down to parkrun in the Bentley next week, OK?

"And maybe I can wear something more appropriate when I do come down next time, OK?

"And leave the really, really expensive Nike trainers at home?" said Sophie.

"OK," said Julian. He took a deep breath and paused, then sheepishly added, "And I think I'll cancel the order for the printed T-shirt".

"Printed T-shirt, what printed T-shirt?" asked Sophie.

"Oh… just a running shirt with some printing on it," said Julian.

"With what exactly?" asked Sophie.

"Oh, just something about me being a really big thing… or something," Julian mumbled.

Wycombe Rye parkrun is very fortunate to have a run director capable of competing with a public address system and often steps in to help out when a strong, loud voice is required. He has often been referred to as Wycombe Rye's 'Mr Shouty Man'. I wondered what would happen if there was a real person who was called Mr Shouty Man and who lived for the day when he could contribute to parkrun, only to be confronted with something that was going to replace him.

==

Mr Shouty Man saves the day...

It was 6.55 a.m., and he was awake. The alarm would go off in five minutes. If he were lucky, he would catch it just in time. He crept out of bed quietly; he woke his daughter with a tap on the head. She got up and got ready. One tea, one coffee and a piece of toast later, they were ready.

He silently put his head around the door of the bedroom.

"WE'RE OFF TO PARKRUN NOW DEAR, SEE YOU AT 10:30!"

The cat jumped off the bed and woke his wife. She buried her head under the pillow and pulled it tight around her ears. The dog barked, and the cat flew under the duvet; his wife let out a scream as the cat clung onto whatever part of her, she could find.

"BYE!"

Mr Shouty Man was on his way to parkrun, his favourite day of the week.

As he drove into the car park, he could see many of

his running friends were already parking their cars. He parked and got out.

Mr Shouty Man saw a few of his friends getting out of their cars on the other side of the car park; some were still in their cars, others were still parking.

"MORNING NICK, MORNING RICHARD, HELLO JO, HELLO LYNDSAY, HIYA CAROLYN, MORNING BOB! HELLO EVERYONE!

They looked up and turned their heads to try to see where the sound was coming from; some squinted. They strained their eyes and saw a person at the far end of the car park, waving.

They waved back.

The volunteers started to arrange the equipment for the parkrun. Cones, flags, signs, tables, chairs, and posts. But today, there was an extra piece, a heavy black box covered in a black hessian cover, and a tripod. No one took much notice, except Mr Shouty Man. He looked at the box and wondered what it was.

He soon forgot about it when he started to think about what he was going to say for the announcement about the new runners' briefing and the briefing about the main briefing and the main briefing and the start-line briefing and the announcement about the volunteer coordinator. This is what Mr Shouty Man was at parkrun for; this was his purpose on a Saturday morning.

"Right then," said today's run director, "let's get everyone sorted. We've got the time-keepers and the scanners over here, people for the finish tokens over there, if you can sort out the funnel and the cones and you can sort out the table and the gazebo, excellent."

Everything was the same as usual, everyone knew their place, and everyone was very organised. Until...

"And this is the new speaker and microphone for the announcements, and this is the list of the marshals for the steps and the split."

Mr Shouty Man stared at the box.

"Right then, Mr Shouty Man, would you like to give the marshal role at the steps a try this week? It might be an interesting change for you."

Mr Shouty man was wide-eyed and silent; he dropped his head and nodded once.

He looked at everyone around him, happily getting on with their tasks. He looked at the shiny new speaker being mounted on the tripod. The run director was fiddling with the knobs and adjusting the aerial. He was blowing into the microphone and counting, 1,2, 1,2

Mr Shouty Man took a deep breath and shrugged his shoulders, then he turned to take the long walk to the furthest part of the course, the marshal post at the steps.

Within five minutes, Mr Shouty Man had reached the steps; it was quiet and a long way from the start of the run. He couldn't see any of the runners, just the late arrivals driving into the car park and the ones who were leaving to find a space somewhere else. He wondered what they would be doing at the briefing. He wondered who would be doing the briefing.

Meanwhile, at the start-line, the run director was still blowing into the microphone and counting. Another person was adjusting the aerial, and a third person was adjusting the knobs.

The black box started to whistle, followed by the

sounds of 1,2 nothing, then 4. It was a run director's nightmare; no one had charged the new speaker!

The first-timers to parkrun and the first-timers to Wycombe Rye were wandering around with no idea of what was going on. The people from the One Can Trust were standing next to an empty blanket with no carrier bags, and no one knew who the volunteer coordinator was. It was turning into a disaster.

As it got to 8.45 a.m., some of the regulars were starting to notice that something wasn't the same as usual. There were murmurings in the masses. People were asking what was going on. People were asking where Mr Shouty Man was.

Then, someone whispered, "Where is Mr Shouty Man?"

Someone else asked, "Have you seen Mr Shouty Man?"

Someone else added, "I thought I'd seen Mr Shouty Man earlier."

A regular runner said, "I think we need Mr Shouty Man," followed by someone else, then someone else.

In no time at all, everyone was yelling, "**WE NEED MR SHOUTY MAN!**"

Six hundred people were shouting, "**WE NEED MR SHOUTY MAN!**"

Meanwhile, over at the steps, Mr Shouty Man was getting ready to marshal the runners. It was so quiet; he wasn't used to that. He stood very still and listened. In the distance, he heard a sound he hadn't heard before. People were shouting his name.

He didn't want to leave his post, but just as he was

thinking about it, a small boy came running across the field. **"WE NEED MR SHOUTY MAN! WE NEED MR SHOUTY MAN!"** he panted.

Mr Shouty Man was overwhelmed. He ran back to the start line. And into the area with all the runners.

They parted as he walked through them. He looked at the run director, and the run director looked at Mr Shouty Man, then at the microphone and shrugged. Mr Shouty Man smiled, turned to the runners, and smiled again.

He took a deep breath and shouted, **"IF YOU ARE NEW TO PARKRUN OR NEW TO WYCOMBE RYE, WELCOME. PLEASE JOIN ME AT THE FRONT FOR THE FIRST TIMERS' BRIEFING."**

When I run at parkrun, I am often amazed when someone passes me pushing a baby buggy with a baby in it, especially the time when the lady pushing the buggy only gave birth to the baby about six months previously. At those times, I briefly wonder if there might be an electric motor linked up to the wheels. This story links the idea of the competitive challenge of the parkrun with someone who is just a little bit too competitive.

===

Steady Eddie

Edward Ready was a very competitive runner. When he joined his local parkrun, he loved the competition, and he loved to get a PB. In the early days of running, he would aim to get a new PB every week. Week after week, it worked; he was getting PBs all the time. Eddie soon learned that as long as he could beat his PB by one or two seconds every week, it was possible to train enough during the week to maintain his progress. Eddie was loving it; he was very competitive.

In the beginning, it was fairly easy, but over time it got a bit harder. Just when he was being recognised as a steady runner, he started to feel the challenge getting more and more difficult.

He was being recognised so much by his fellow runners that some of them started referring to him as 'Steady Eddie'. He even got a mention in the briefings at the beginning of the weekly run, and their run reports often mentioned the exploits of their local 'Steady Eddie'.

But eventually, the inevitable happened; Eddie started to struggle to get his PBs. It was no longer possible to hang back and check his watch to ensure he only beat his time by a couple of seconds; he now had to run hard and sprint at the end to get his PB. Eddie was getting desperate.

One day, whilst attempting to run the steps, he was almost passed by a runner pushing a pushchair! He was mortified, and not only that, the man with the pushchair ran up a different route, avoiding the steps altogether!

Eddie was in a state, he had to maintain his status, and he had to maintain his PBs, but how to achieve it when he had reached his maximum speed and best PB? Eddie got thinking… and thought about the man and the pushchair…

In normal circumstances, Eddie was a very nice, kind man, but his competitive nature sometimes got the better of him. He was also very practical, some would say ingenious, and these characteristics sometimes got mixed up and made Eddie behave in strange ways.

He decided to see his sister, ask for her advice and see if it was possible to take Eva in her pushchair.

"You can borrow Eva's pushchair, but she's too young at the moment to be pushed round on Saturday," said his sister, Rita.

Strangely, Eddie was fine with that and took the pushchair away.

Eddie took the pushchair to his workshop; he had an idea that he wanted to test out at next week's parkrun.

The next week Eddie arrived at parkrun bright and early; he parked and produced his newly acquired pushchair from the car. It wasn't a particularly cold morning, but there was a big blanket on the buggy covering up something on the seat.

He took the buggy for a test run. He felt good, the buggy felt good, he was running around quite quickly, it didn't feel like he was being held back by the pushchair at all. But he kept away from his parkrun friends, just in case they took much notice. Eventually, some of his friends turned up.

"Hi Eddie, we didn't know you had a baby."

"I don't; my sister has one," he replied, in a technically correct sort of way. "I'm just trying the buggy out this week," he added, being very economical with the truth.

"You'll have to push hard to maintain your PBs with a buggy to push," said one of his friends.

As usual, the briefing session mentioned Eddie, and everyone gave him a clap. He accepted the applause graciously and then got ready for the start.

Eddie held the pushchair tightly then put his thumb on a small lever under the handlebar. He felt the pushchair move slightly. The starter counted them down... 3, 2, 1 go!

Everyone set off; Eddie started at a slow, steady pace; he didn't want to go off too fast; he didn't want to draw attention to himself.

After 1 km, Eddie was feeling good. He was on target for a good time, but not too good that it would look spectacular. He jogged along with his finger adjusting the little lever under the handlebar; everything was going to plan... until...

Eddie came up along the other runner with the pushchair and slowly eased past. The other runner was impressed.

"Nice one, Eddie," he said, "you're doing really well with the pushchair. They really don't slow you down too much, do they?"

"No, they don't," said Eddie, feeling slightly embarrassed.

"Go for it, Eddie," said the other runner, as he gave Eddie an encouraging slap on the shoulder.

Eddie was just about to thank the other pushchair runner when he felt the nudge travel all the way down his arm to his hand, to his thumb, and to the lever, which was controlling the speed that the pushchair was travelling at. And the lever got stuck!

Within a second, Eddie went from saying "Thanks mate" to "Whoooaaa!" as the pushchair started pulling him along the course. Suddenly, a controllable pushchair acted like an out-of-control supermarket trolley linked to the rope from the water-skiing boat!

Eddie was in danger of beating his PB by minutes, not seconds. At the speed he was going, he was probably going to break the course record, maybe the world record! Everything started to come rushing towards him: the other runners, the trees, the steps! How would he negotiate the alternative route for pushchairs at the speed he was going? How would he get past the steps at the speed he was going? He had to think fast; maybe he could slow the pushchair down by digging his heels in a bit? He tried, but the wet ground was only making it worse by leaving a pair of muddy lines all the way round the football field.

Eddie was speeding round the parkrun course, and everyone was looking at him in amazement as he flew by them. Eddie looked at them with a look of surprise and embarrassment as he tried to run at the speed of the pushchair, desperately trying to pull the lever to slow the pushchair down.

He approached the steps and swerved to go up the alternative route; it just about worked, but now Eddie was flying past the runners coming in the other direction. He started overtaking runners who were really quite fast. He started to catch up with the leading runner. How would he explain beating the fastest runner and coming home first in parkrun when he was pushing a pushchair!

Maybe he could pull harder on the pushchair and reduce the power; it would take a lot of effort, but it must be worth it. He started to pull against the pushchair as he continued to pass the other runners. As he reached the end of the Dyke, he could feel the pushchair slowing; it started to feel like it did at the beginning, then he could feel it was getting heavy, he could feel the weight of the lump under the blanket that the others thought was Eva feeling very heavy. He was now going very slowly, so slowly that other runners were passing him. He was even passed by the other pushchair runner.

"Come on, Eddie, you can do it!" they shouted.

The last 1 km was the hardest he'd ever run. Everyone he'd passed earlier was overtaking him. By the end of the run, he was just a few seconds away from his last PB. The end of the consecutive PBs had arrived; he could no longer call himself Steady Eddie. As he crawled across the line, he was exhausted; he'd tried harder than ever before but still hadn't managed to achieve a PB.

The run director came across to commiserate with him. "Interesting run Eddie, I'm not sure if your niece Eva Ready was a help or a hindrance to you today?" he said, with a knowing hint in his voice.

"To be honest, it was more 'Ever-Ready' than Eva Ready that made the difference today, I'm afraid."

"Not to worry," said the run director, "maybe leave Eva at home next week and come along and pace for a change; we need some steady running, and you could be the ideal man for that.

I am always surprised at how a disparate group of people who come together at eight in the morning can complete the whole parkrun setup in as little as 30 minutes without so much as a few instructions and a brief explanation. I've known many people who would have needed much more time to plan for this type of activity, and this story is about one of those types of people.

==================================

The Funnel Manager

Martin was a parkrunner with over fifty runs to his name and a regular, but not frequent, volunteer.

As an experienced technical manager in a multi-national company, he came along to parkrun to meet a few people, and have a nice run and get away from a world of spreadsheets and numbers that was his life during the week. When he volunteered, he took one of the easier outposts on the course with a few cones and sometimes a bit of tape. He enjoyed encouraging other runners and getting feedback from runners as they ran past, saying, "Thank you, Marshal."

By the time he got back to the finish line with the cones from his marshalling point, most of the equipment was put away, and he would say his goodbyes and turn up again the following week to run.

But, when he'd put his name down to volunteer the next time, there were only a few spaces left, and he inadvertently put his name down for funnel manager.

A funnel manager is an important role at parkrun because the arrival of runners over the finish line is a lot faster than the ability of one person, the token hander-outer, with the help of the token hander-outer support role, to give everyone a token. It's therefore necessary to queue the runners in finish order to ensure they get the right time token for the time that they finished the run. The finishing funnel is a system that has evolved over the years from a single line to a dual system to a three-lane system with queue markers to keep the runners in position.

The funnel manager's primary role is to ensure that the person handing out the token gives the correct time token to the correct runner, which is a challenge, especially with hundreds of people in the queue. So, Martin took extra notice of the funnel system when he finished his run the previous week and made some notes about what he needed to do when it was his turn to be in charge.

He then checked all the parkrun roles on the list and noticed they were keepers, coordinators, supporters, and plain old marshals and realised that the funnel manager role was the only 'manager' role you could volunteer for, so he assumed this had added responsibility on the day.

By the week before, the gravity of the role was starting to worry him. He started to wonder how many runners would cross the line and what the flow would be from the first to the last. As a statistician at heart, he knew there would be a bit of variation, but the more he thought about the variables, the more he wondered how it would all work. What if the number of runners was greater than expected? What if they stood too far apart in the funnel? What if the funnel wasn't long enough? What if he needed to specify an extra funnel? What if the token hander-outer was slower at handing out than normal? What if they dropped the tokens?

It was six days before the day that he would be funnel manager, and he was starting to panic. He was thinking about what he had seen on Saturday; where the funnel started, where it finished... how long was that? He couldn't remember. He'd have to do a calculation. How wide was the funnel? He thought about the width of the funnel, then the average width of a runner, remembered that the average time to complete was getting slower, would there be people who were wider than average? Ignore the average, he thought, I'll make it as wide as possible. Then he remembered buggies. Then the double buggies. By Tuesday night, he was starting to have nightmares.

His nightmares were all about funnels. In his worst one he woke up in a cold sweat thinking about a pile of runners all tangled up in a heap with all the netting wound around them with lots of arms and hands stretching out trying to grasp a token. He realised that he had no choice, he had to create a spreadsheet!

Martin spent the rest of the week filling in and updating his spreadsheet; he'd work before work, during work and after work. His final spreadsheet was a masterpiece. He looked at historical patterns of the total numbers of runners in previous years and projected a number that he thought would complete the course. He then thought about the arrival times from the fastest to the slowest and built a bell curve that predicted the minute when the highest numbers of runners would cross the line and a cumulative graph showing the time when the greatest numbers of runners would be in the funnel.

He built in all possible scenarios: runners not passing through the funnel, runners spacing out too much, runners not concentrating when being given the token and slowing the hander-out down, runners falling over, single buggies, a smaller number of double buggies, under 11s, and dogs, lots of dogs with short and long leads... He thought he'd included everything.

By the end of Friday night, he pushed 'save' on the spreadsheet and printed it out, all ten pages.

On Saturday morning, he arrived in the car park at ten past eight and noticed that the early volunteers were already transferring the equipment from the storage area to the start line area. He noticed that people were already lugging the large rolls of orange fencing and the fence poles to make the funnel towards the start line.

That's funny, he thought to himself, *how do they know how many they'll need, or where to put them... or how far apart they need to be?*

He started to worry; he quickly parked the car then ran to the car park machine. He typed in his vehicle registration number and was about to put his 50p in the slot when he realised, he needed to put £1 for going over two hours.

He let out an "Arrghh!" as he ran back to the car... where is that £1 coin, he shouted at himself. He couldn't find it... "Arrghh!" he shouted again; it was a £5 note. It was no use; he'd have to get change from the Lido. He locked the car and started running round to the Lido. He saw a couple of young volunteers carrying more fencing to the start line.

"If you can hang on, I'll be with you in a minute; I've got a spreadsheet!" he called out, his voice drowning out as he ran up the steps of the Lido to the reception area.

"Can I get some change please?" he said breathlessly.

"Sorry, pet, I'm afraid we're cashless here since last week; you could try the café, through those doors."

"Right, OK, thanks!" Martin ran through the double doors to the café in a very hurried way.

"Morning, I'm just opening up. Can I get you a coffee or maybe a cappuccino, or are you a flat white?"

"No, no coffee, thanks!" he panted.

"Tea then, I've got builder's, Earl Grey or Darjeeling?"

"No, I don't want tea or coffee!"

"Oh, well, this *is* a café," the owner said, a little indignantly.

"I'm sorry, I need some change for the car park."

"Well, they should have told you at the reception that we're all cashless now."

"Arrghh!" said Martin… he was losing time. *Mobile phone, they must take mobile parking*, he thought to himself.

He ran outside, calling to the volunteers who were unwinding the funnel's fencing and placing it in line with the other volunteers.

"I'll be with you in a minute; hang on, I've got a spreadsheet for you…" They looked at each other puzzled and continued to unroll the fencing.

Martin ran back to the car. Keys, door, now, where was the phone. "Arrghh!" WHERE WAS THE PHONE!

Found it, now how to pay.

Fifteen minutes later, having shouted many words that are not usually spoken in the car park preceding a parkrun, Martin had spent £1 and managed to pay the car park for the time required.

He ran back to the car to leave his things and pulled a second 50p from his pocket. He looked at two coins in his hand.

"Arrghh!" he shouted.

It was now 8.45 a.m., and he ran to the start line to see the run director; the young volunteers he saw earlier were walking past him. He looked at them in surprise as he approached the run director.

"I'm so sorry, the car park machine. No £1 coin, cashless, mobile…" he blurted out a stream of random words. "The funnel, now, I've got this spreadsheet, do we have time?" he hurriedly opened his sheets of paper and presented them to the run director.

"Morning Martin, actually, you're just in time; the funnel's already for you over there. If you can pick up the instructions and the volunteer bib, you'll be in action from around nine-thirty. By the way, you do know that you can buy the car park ticket when you leave the car, don't you? See you later."

Martin looked at the run director, his jaw dropped, he looked at his sheet, then looked at the funnel all set up; it was perfect.

He looked at his spreadsheet, sighed, folded it neatly and, putting it in his pocket with a gentle tap on his coat where it was safe he thought, *I'll keep it for next time, just in case.*

In early 2020 a contact was created via Facebook between people at the Whangarei parkrun in New Zealand and the Wycombe Rye parkrun. I was talking to a New Zealand friend about this and mentioned the town of Whangarei. He had no idea of where I was talking about, and in the end, I had to spell the name out. "W-H-A-N-G-A-R-E-I." "Oh!" he said, "Fon Gar Ray." This story imagines a situation where a visitor from New Zealand comes to Wycombe Rye.

===

The important visitor from New Zealand

Bob is a dedicated parkrunner from Whangarei parkrun in New Zealand, which, as everyone in New Zealand knows, uses the Maori pronunciation so that Whangarei is pronounced 'Fon Gar Ray' and not 'Wang Gar Rye" as many people in the UK would assume.

Nick is the run director for the Wycombe Rye parkrun in the UK, which, as everyone in the UK knows, is a place in High Wycombe which is pronounced 'High Wick Ham' and not 'High Why Combe Be' as many people outside the UK would assume.

During the Covid pandemic, various members of the Wycombe Rye parkrun and Whangarei parkrun made contact via Facebook and shared many stories together; many people found it interesting that two places many miles apart sounded so similar, Whangarei and Wycombe Rye.

Now Bob, was a great traveller, and when the time was right, he booked a trip to the UK to see some friends in Loughborough, Leicestershire. He noticed that the

Wycombe Rye parkrun wasn't too far away from London's Heathrow airport and decided to see if he could stop off at the Wycombe Rye parkrun on the Saturday morning before travelling up to Loughborough. He contacted the run director to let him know. Nick was so excited. He really wanted to meet someone from Whangarei and introduce him to all the Wycombe Rye runners.

So it was that on the Saturday morning at eight-thirty, Bob turned into the car park at the Wycombe Lido; he parked and got his ticket. Nick had briefed the volunteers to look out for a Bob from Wang Gar Rye in New Zealand. Bob looked around and spotted a volunteer; he walked over and greeted them.

"Hey man, I'm Bob from Fon Gar Ray; I'm looking for a Nick who's in charge of the Why Combe Be Rye parkrun."

The volunteer looked and stared. "Fon Gar What? You want a Nick who's in charge of what?"

"Fon Gar Ray, I'm looking for Nick the run director; I'm Bob from New Zealand

"Ah, right, wow, another Bob, that's, that's amazing" the penny had dropped slightly. "You want to see Nick the run director? Sure, I can find him for you."

The volunteer ran off to find Nick.

"Nick, Nick, there's a bloke called Bob from New Zealand, but he's not from Wang Gar Rye, he's from Fon Gar Ray, or something like that."

"You sure he's not from Wang Gar Rye?" asked Nick

"No, it's definitely not that, he said Fon Gar Ray, although, to be honest, he might be in the wrong place, he kept talking about 'why combes and bees and ryes'."

"Well, we'll have to keep our eyes open for Bob from Wang Gar Rye, he should be here by now, and I've got a special announcement to make to introduce him and all these New Zealand Flags to wave. You go look out for the real Bob, and I'll go and talk to the other Bob."

Nick made his way over to see the other Bob.

"Hello, Bob, lovely to meet you, you're here from New Zealand, where from exactly?" he turned his ear to listen carefully to the other Bob's response.

"I'm Bob from Fon Gar Ray parkrun in New Zealand; I'm really pleased to be able to join you guys at the Why Combe Bee Rye parkrun; this place looks skux today. He gave a thumbs-up at the same time he said 'skux'.

Nope, Nick thought to himself, *not even close; and not only was he the wrong Bob, but he was also in the wrong place, and now he thought the place sucks.* Nick shrugged his shoulders.

"OK, Bob, well, welcome to our parkrun; you can be our second honoured guest from New Zealand. Look we've even got flags!" Nick turned to the box of flags the volunteers were unpacking.

Bob was distracted from what Nick had said and was looking at the flags.

"So, you've got some people from Australia here as well, have you?" said Bob, nodding towards the flags.

"Australia. You mean they're not New Zealand flags? Nick exclaimed.

"Nope, too many stars, mate, and they're white, not red."

Now that really does skux, thought Nick.

It was getting towards briefing time.

Nick got the volunteers to go out on a final hunt looking for the real Bob.

His instructions were clear: "He'll probably look a bit lost, and he's bound to be wearing black."

Everyone in the UK knew that New Zealanders wore a black t-shirt when in the UK or the parkrun 100 shirt when they were at parkrun. In the meantime, Nick got a message to all the flag-wavers to make sure they waved the flag very vigorously when the real Bob turned up, just in case he spotted that the flags had the six stars of Australia and not the four red stars of New Zealand.

With fifteen minutes to go, Nick decided to use the PA system to make a request.

"Would Bob from Wang Gar Rye parkrun in New Zealand please contact Nick the run director as soon as possible? Thank you."

Bob took no notice of the announcement; why would he, especially as he was busy introducing himself to the locals and talking about how far he'd travelled from Fon Gar Ray and how skux everyone was looking.

Eventually, for Nick, the time ran out, the real Bob couldn't be found; the other Bob had made friends with everyone, and it was time for the runners' briefing.

He turned on the PA. "Good morning, everyone, and welcome to Wycombe Rye parkrun."

Bob looked up. What was Wick Ham Rye, he thought to himself?

"I'm afraid we have some bad news and some good news for you this morning. The bad news is that our honoured visitor, Bob from Wang Gar Rye parkrun in New Zealand, hasn't been able to make it here today…"

The runners let out a disappointed "Ohhh!"

"But we have got another Bob who has come all the way from Fon Gar Ray, which is also in New Zealand!"

"Hooray!" yelled all the parkrunners.

"Now as we know, New Zealand is a very long way away, even further away than Australia, which is a long way away," said Nick.

"Only if you fly via Dubai!" shouted out one of the runners.

"What?" said Nick.

"Or Singapore, or Bali!" shouted two more.

"But not if you fly via the States!" shouted the first person.

Nick started to look frustrated.

"Or South America!" shouted someone else.

There's a general murmur of agreement from various other runners and discussion on the various ways people have travelled out east or west if they went via the States.

"What about Japan?"

Nick took a deep breath.

"Look, OK, I grant you, New Zealand isn't quite as far as Australia if you fly from anywhere in the Americas, but it is a long way away from anywhere between here and Australia, so we want to thank the other Bob for coming so far to join us today.

"As you know, we've been in contact with Bob from Wang Gar Rye on Facebook for many months, and it's a shame that he can't be here, but aren't we lucky to have the other Bob replace the real Bob on this special New

Zealand themed day?"

"What about the Australian flags?" asked someone from the front.

"Shhhh!" said Nick, frowning at the person who asked and giving a stare that meant don't ask again.

Meanwhile, Bob walked forward and had a word with Nick. Nick shook Bob's hand, and they had a laugh.

Nick turned back to the runners and lifted the microphone to his mouth.

"Special announcement: I'm very pleased to say that we have some good news and no bad news to share with you."

"Hooray!" shout nearly all the parkrunners.

"But what about these Australian flags?" asked the person who was not concentrating on the announcements.

"Shhhh!" said a group of runners standing next to him.

"I've just been advised that the other Bob from Fon Gar Ray is actually the *real* Bob from Wang Gar Rye!"

The parkrunners give out another loud cheer, except the runner looking at the Australian flags who was still asking what to do with them.

Nick turned to Bob and gave him a wink and a smile, then turned to the flag-wavers to encourage them to wave the flags faster.

The briefing over, everyone turned to walk to the start line.

Nick and Bob talk to each other on the way to the start line.

"Well, Nick, that session was skux."

"Are you sure skux is a good thing, Bob? It sounds

like another word that doesn't mean good."

"OK Nick, just for you: it's been a really cool day; I just hope I don't have any more problems like that during my stay in the UK.

"Let's hope so, Bob," said Nick.

"Now all I need is someone to help me with directions to 'Lou goo ber oooo ga' in 'Lei Ses Ter Shire' do you know anyone who can help?"

"To be honest, Bob, if I were you, I'd type it into Google."

One of the nicest things about parkrun is the support that volunteers give the runners and that the runners give the volunteers. When a group of runners turned up with their names on the front of their running vests, it was more encouraging for the runners when the volunteers could shout support for the runner using the runner's name. I wondered how this might be for someone who was a volunteer rather than a runner.

==

Bobble and Trevor make friends

"It's OK, there's no one there. You get the ticket, and I'll go and park the car," said his mum as he jumped out of the car.

He ran to the ticket machine and got the ticket, then ran back to the car, fumbling with the door handle in his rush to get back in.

They were early; they needed to be early to get ready without the crowds. They needed to have a chat about what they were going to do and how they were going to do it.

As the time drew nearer, people started arriving and the car park got busier. It was time.

He put on his hat and made sure it was pulled down. He got out of the car and waited for his mum to walk around. They made their way to the large group of people setting up all the equipment.

His mum walked up to the man in the blue-and-grey run director's jacket. He was the man she was told to go and see. She caught his eye and he walked over to her.

"Hello, I'm Jayne, I spoke to you in the week." She

raised her eyebrows at the run director and then looked down at her son who was standing right in front of her, his eyes glued to the floor.

"We thought maybe you could use an extra volunteer this week?" her voice raising at the end to turn her statement into a pleading question.

"Yes, right. Well. As I said we don't have any specific roles this week, but it would be great if we could have someone to help one of our volunteers on the course, would that be, OK?" said the run director.

"That would be great, that would be really good wouldn't it?" She knelt down in front of her son who was still looking at the floor.

"OK then," said the run director, "You hang on here a second and I'll find Trevor, then you'll have a walk over to the section where you can set out some cones and tape then wait for the runners to come around."

They waited for Trevor.

Trevor came over and introduced himself to Jayne and Jayne explained that her son was a bit shy but that he was looking forward to volunteering. She'd got pretty good at mouthing sentences to people without saying certain words so it wasn't obvious what she was saying about her son, but Trevor got the message that his new helper wasn't going to be a chatterbox, which was fine for Trevor; he could talk for England!

"OK then," said Trevor, "let's go and set up the course, all right?"

Trevor thought he heard a quiet "OK" from somewhere under the thick woollen bobble hat that he was wearing, but he wasn't too sure.

"You know what," said Trevor, "that's such a great hat you're wearing I'm going to call you Bobble. Is that OK?" Trevor had a way of making people feel more relaxed, or so he thought.

The hat nodded slightly so Trevor took that as a yes.

Trevor chatted all the way over to the section where they were going to set up but didn't hear a lot of noise from under the hat, apart from the odd "yes" or "OK" but, he soon found that his little helper was very good at setting out cones and putting tapes around trees so within a few minutes they were working like a real team.

"Ok, then Bobble," said Trevor, "we've done all our work, we just have to wait for the runners to come round now."

They leant against a tree looking back across the park. They could see the runners assembling for the start and then saw them start to round the bend and then back towards where they were standing.

"Get ready now," said Trevor, "we need to clap the runners and give them lots of encouragement." He wasn't sure quite how Bobble was going to do that, but he was all enthusiastic now and hoped that some of it would rub off on his new little friend.

As the first runner approached, they started clapping, and then the second followed soon after.

When the third runner approached, he looked up at Trevor and his friend.

"Thank you Marshal," he said, panting and breathing deeply.

The fourth, fifth and six went racing by all thanking the volunteers with a loud, "Thank you Marshal!"

Bobble started clapping vigorously; he was really enjoying this. Trevor could see that he was enjoying himself as he looked down and saw his little helper looking up at him with a great big smile.

They spent the next hour cheering and clapping the runners out and back as they completed their runs. When the tail walkers finished, they packed up the cones, put the tape in the box and started walking back to the finish line.

As they got towards the finish line, Trevor took over the carrying of the cones as his little helper saw his mum.

"We'll have to get you signed up to get you volunteering every week if you enjoy it so much," he said to Bobble.

The little boy saw his mum and started skipping towards her.

"What's your real name so I put you down on the list?" Trevor shouted out after him.

"It's Marshal!" shouted the little boy.

Queues are a key feature at the beginning of parkrun. There are queues for toilets, and for the car park ticket machine. This story is about a parkrunner who starts his competitive activities before he starts his run and meets a man in the queue who is probably more dedicated to parkrun than most.

==

Christopher, the impatient man in the queue

Christopher was an impatient man in a queue. So he sometimes skipped the queue in the car park and went to the ticket machine at the entrance to the swimming pool; it was a bit further away but sometimes faster in the long run. Today, the car park queue looked like it might be short enough.

He joined the queue, then looked to the front to see what the first person was doing. Someone joined the queue behind. Within seconds, the queue was twice as long, and someone was already shouting from the back.

"You need to push the green button first, then put the registration number in, then put the money in!"

The two people at the back sighed, and started to walk off; they obviously couldn't remember their registration so were off to find their cars.

"You could take a photo of the car," shouted someone else in the queue, as the people walked away. "I always do that, it saves me having to remember every week," they said to someone else in the queue, who said 'thank you' in a not-kind-of-listening sort of way.

Meanwhile the next person had their ticket, and three more people joined the end of the queue, and Christopher moved one step nearer to the front.

"So, what are the steps like, I hear they are steep?" asked a person next to Christopher whom he assumed to be a parkrun tourist.

"Well, they aren't exactly steep," said Christopher, "it's just that there are a few of them and they are quite spaced out, and there can be a bit of a muddy patch just before you get to them."

Someone else in the queue offered more advice: "I always try to keep running and take large strides."

Someone else joined in and suggested following a buggy up the alternative route and someone else reminded the other person that it wasn't the steps, it was the long drag of thirty metres after the steps that was the real killer.

Three more people joined the queue and Christopher moved one step nearer the machine.

Christopher noticed someone ahead of him in the queue had on a pair of brand-new training shoes and a piece of A4 paper with six bar codes printed on it neatly folded (*It won't look like that when they finish and try to get it scanned,* he thought to himself) and a full water bottle, iPhone strapped to their arm and wires from the phone tucked into a baseball cap, which was finally attached to some headphones. He guessed that it was their first time to parkrun, first time to the Lido car park and first time to the ticket machine. They probably didn't have a 50p or know their car's registration and they probably hadn't used the ticket machine before.

Christopher was beginning to think it might have been the wrong day to join this queue.

One of his regular running pals walked up to join the queue, "Morning, how are we today?" he asked.

"Not bad, couple of runs this week and a ride out on the bike last night, legs a bit sore, how are you?"

"Not bad either, thanks; just talking to these new folks about the steps." He turned to introduce the others in the queue.

"Ah yes, the steps, what's the path like round that section today, many standing puddles in the mud?"

Christopher chatted to the visitors about various other elements of the route with arms hoisted high up pointing in various directions in front and behind trying to give two people with no idea of the topography of the Rye an idea of which direction they'll be running and the types of surface they'll be running on, interspersed with a few glances to the front of the line to see how much progress they'd made.

Another regular whom he hadn't seen for a while approached the queue.

"Morning, feeling confident today?"

"Not today," he said, "I got back from a business trip last week and haven't been out this week; had a big meal last night and one glass of wine too many. Can't believe I made it down here this morning; can't think of anything else that would get me out of bed on a chilly Saturday morning like parkrun though. See you at the start line," he said and continued walking off.

Christopher assumed he was on his way to the shorter queue in the Lido; he was starting to feel agitated.

"So," the visitor tourist continued, "there are very few hills here is that right?"

The visitor then explained that Wycombe Rye, apart from the steps, and the slope down to the football field, was known to be fairly flat and that they were hoping for a good time because of the lack of hills. He also hoped that the wide-open start would help them to get running without too much traffic.

He then told Christopher that even though Wycombe Rye started with a 'W', which you would think was quite a rare letter in the parkrun A-Z, there were 44 other places that started with 'W' in the UK. Their local parkrun at Haigh Woodland Park in Wigan was a bit hilly and, unfortunately, started with an 'H' rather than a 'W' so they were only at Wycombe Rye to help with the 'Personal Best Poem' that they had started writing a year ago. Apparently, he needed a time which would rhyme with 'W' (something to do with wanting to include the initial letter from his name) so anything that ended in a '2' would be OK but if it could be a '22' it would be even better. He thought maybe 22:22 would be in target, which would be amazing, but failing that any 2 would be OK...except 12.

He was also keen to have a name that he could use that rhymed with Wigan, so Wycombe was ideal for the other rhyme in the poem. It had been quite a trip down and he was in two minds whether to make it but luckily, he was able to include a visit to the local chair museum and a visit to the first multi-screen cinema in the UK at Cressex—now called the Empire Cinema, which was very nearby, so it was actually quite a worthwhile trip.

Christopher was impressed by their knowledge of the course, and even more so with their dedication to parkrun associated activities but he was now wondering if they were just being polite, when they seemed so interested in the detailed description he'd just given them, about the course.

They were nearly at the machine now. Three more people joined the end of the queue.

The regular with whom he'd had the discussion about the business trip and the wine walked past back to his car; the Lido queue was obviously a lot shorter than usual. He gave Christopher a glance and a look that said, *You should've used the Lido ticket machine* before running off to put his ticket on his windscreen. Christopher now knew that he made the wrong choice and was desperately hoping that he'll have his ticket before his friend walks back past him for the third time whilst he remained in the queue.

But he was in luck, the person ahead of him was a regular, she knew her registration and has a shiny new 50p piece. She got her ticket and then Christopher was at the front of the queue.

Within a flash, he had his ticket in hand; he turned to his visitor friend to say, 'bye and see you later'. But horror! He's standing in front of the machine with eyes wide open looking like someone seeing the Wycombe Rye steps for the first time! He obviously wasn't listening to all the helpful comments earlier on and no doubt thinking more about his rhyming poem with double u's and 2's, and his trips to the chair museum and cinema, than concentrating on how to use the machine.

Christopher hesitated for a second; the adrenalin was pumping. His first bit of competition for the morning was about to kick off but the need to help a fellow park runner in distress was starting to kick in also. How would he feel if he abandoned his tourist friend who he only knew as the man from Wigan with a name that begins with 'W'? If he were running and he fell over he knew that he would stop and help but does a slight delay in getting his ticket mean the same? It probably ranked the same as seeing a runner with a shoelace undone; an inconvenience maybe, but not life threatening surely, unless they tripped! Christopher's mind was made up.

Christopher felt compelled to stay and help a fellow park runner. But was there be a chance that he could still save face AND help the park runner in distress? If only his friend has parked at the back of the car park, he might have a chance. He felt as though it might be worth just checking to see where his friend is. He might still have time...

But no, he glances across the car park to check, but he too has started to compete early; he's jogging back... *Damn it!* thinks Christopher.

At least he could use the tourist as an excuse for why he was so delayed at the main ticket machine when the inevitable question came up in the discussion later on, rather than admit to a momentary lapse of concentration in the car park when he arrived.

He turned to his tourist friend.

"Now then," he said, "what's your car's registration?"

Volunteers that are thrown together at the early morning briefing go off to various places to set up the course. I wondered what it would be like if two random people with different views on how important their task was were put together at an important place like the split.

==

Petra and Jonathan Manage the Split

The allocation of volunteer roles at parkrun is either a guarantee of a specific role or a bit of a lottery, which is interesting because that same difference between two extremes can sometimes be the same as the people who are allocated to work with each other on a Saturday morning.

So it was with Jonathan and Petra; two individuals who were introduced to each other as they were handed the trolley complete with cones, tape, kilometre markers and instructions for the marshal point they call the 'split' at the Wycombe Rye parkrun.

The split is an important part of the route because it's the point where runners that are on their way out onto the football fields meet up with the faster runners who are on their return to the finish line, having completed the loop of the football fields and tackled the famous steps.

Added to that is the important arrow at the top of the waterfall which directs runners to turn left (following the path down the hill to the football field) rather than jump the wall and fall thirty feet to crash onto the rocks below where life and limb would be extinguished and broken, in a mass of other runners who had also failed to follow the path or turned right.

There's also one other feature of marshalling at the split: two important kilometre markers on the outbound and return parts of the course.

This is truly one important marshal stage which should not be attempted without reading the instructions carefully and fastidiously. The slightest error in the position of a cone, the direction of an arrow or the location of a 2km or 3km marker could have consequences covering nearly every scenario in the run director's failure-mode handbook. This is exactly what was going through Petra's mind as she walked across to the steps with her newly allocated partner, Jonathan.

"So, Petra?" said Jonathan, "that's an interesting name… your parents fans of Blue Peter, or somit?

"Pardon…? what? Oh no… not Blue Peter. They were archaeologists in Jordan, I'm named after the city."

"I thought Jordan was a model…" said Jonathan, clearly mixing up the names.

"No, the city of Petra, in Jordan."

"Ah, right…" said Jonathan, having learned two new things already that morning.

"So, have you marshalled this point on the route before?" asked Petra.

"Nope, I stood by the trees at the playground last time, just a couple of cones and a bit of tape to put up round the tree, piece of cake… guess this will be the same."

Having read the instructions already, Petra was starting to feel a little anxious about her volunteer colleague. The instructions, the detailed diagram, the position and exact number of cones was starting to worry her but as a dedicated runner with over a hundred parkruns to her name, the most important thing she was worried about was the position of the 2km marker on the way to the split.

Over the years, she'd often run the route and noticed that the 2km marker was in a different place every week. On a 5 km route it wasn't that much of an issue to make a fuss about, but she sometimes felt as though it really *should* be in the right place. After all, the position of the 2km marker was important to judge your pace for the 2nd k but also to know if your 3k split was on target. There is nothing more irritating to a hardened runner than having to process a difference in your split time between what you can remember your time as being when you passed the marker to what your £300 Garmin watch is telling you at the end of the run. This was her chance to make sure the marker was in the correct place, in addition to a couple of other things she'd noticed on the instructions.

"So, have you got the run director's mobile phone plugged into your phone?" she asked.

"Not yet, I'll do it later," said Jonathan.

"OK, and which bits shall we set up first? I was going to sugg…" Petra started to say.

"Tell, you what, I'll go and do the markers and the arrow, and you set out the cones, OK?" said Jonathan.

Petra, felt rushed; she knew the cones were important, not just the spacing but the positioning and the special single cone in the middle of the return path to stop people going the wrong way round the loop, but would her new friend know exactly where to put the 2km marker? She suspected that he wasn't as focussed as she was about the correct position and was sure he'd just wander along the route to a random place on the right and hammer it in in a soft spot, rather than the correct spot that she had identified.

She had to think quickly. "Tell you what," she said, "why don't *you* place the cones in the general area, and *I'll* go and do the markers. I think I know exactly where it needs to go, right down there. Then when I get back, we can position the cones in the exact locations together unless you want to walk all the way down there and put the marker in?" She stood on her tiptoes and pointed with her arm in such a way that it made an arch, suggesting, she hoped, that it was a long way away.

"Okey dokey," said Jonathan, quickly, "you want to do the 3 k and the arrow when you get back as well?"

Petra was starting to feel good; this was going better than expected. By the time she'd got back from the 2k marker she could check the cones and give Jonathan more instructions, then go and hang the arrow. She wanted to make sure the arrow was easy to see from the path so that there was no chance any runner could mistake the gap in the fence as a possible route. She walked off to find the correct spot for the 2k marker.

On her way back she could see Jonathan had created a few piles of cones in various places and was sitting on the seat looking at his phone.

"That's great," she said, "I'll be back in a minute to help you set them out."

She jogged off down the hill to place the arrow; a few walkers were taking a keen interest in what she was doing, they were also leaning over the fence looking at the waterfall. She hoped they were not going to stand in front of her arrow after she had placed it in position. She decided not to say anything and ran off back to where Jonathan was seated.

They then spent the next ten minutes placing, replacing, adjusting and measuring the lines of the cones, taking it in turns to stand where the runners would come from in both directions, before finally — after a couple of final adjustments and repositions of the cones at the end of the line — placing the single solitary cone in the middle of the return path like the placement of the fairy on a Christmas tree. They stood back. Petra leaned forward and moved the cone a couple of inches to the left. Jonathan looked at Petra, then the cone, then moved the cone slightly back a bit. They looked at each other, "Happy with that?" said Petra.

"Yeeess, I think so," he said as he went to move forward. He stopped.

"No, that's fine, it's just fine. I don't think anyone is going to go that way."

They sat in the chair waiting for the start. They heard the start and took up positions. They stood either side of the path as the runners approached. "Well done, Keep to the left. Well done!" they shouted.

As the first runner approached, Jonathan moved onto the track, "Well done, keep left!"

Petra could see that he was directly in the line of sight of the first cone. She was starting to feel pleased that she hadn't made the final adjustment to the single cone because they couldn't see it anyway.

But as she looked down the hill towards the arrow she started to panic. There were walkers standing in front of the arrows, clapping! Every disaster was flashing through her mind. She imagined runners stopping, turning right, going over the wall or attempting the small opening down to the waterfall. She summoned all her strength, running down towards the lead runner, approaching the arrow. "KEEP LEFT! TURN LEFT! KEEP LEFT!"

"Thank you, Marshal. Oh, hello Petra," said a runner, just passing her, "don't worry, that's Kieran, he knows which way to go."

A stream of runners started to run past her, all turning left at the end.

"Thank you Marshal," they all repeated.

She started to relax… but then panicked again. The single cone! She turned round. Jonathan was standing in the middle of the path and he hadn't moved the cone! Petra started running back up the hill. She wasn't dressed for running and had the wrong shoes on. She was starting to puff! She glanced to the left; the first runner was approaching the split; he was much faster than her and was beginning to overtake. There was only one thing for it.

Once again, she breathed in deeply: "JONATHAN, THE CONE. REMOVE THE CONE!"

Jonathan turned round just as the runner approached "Whoops-a-daisy, there you go," as he stood back to let the first runner past. "Well done, good running, don't forget to keep left!"

Don't forget to keep left? Petra fumed at herself,

"don't forget to move the cone*!"* she fumed again.

She walked up to Jonathan who was busy clapping "Well done. Keep to the left, well done!" he shouted excitedly to the runners.

Petra stood and looked at Jonathan in a kind of "what do you think I've been doing for the last ten minutes," kind of a way.

"Careful Petra, you're standing in the middle of the path," shouted Jonathan as a group of runners came bounding into her. They all had their heads down looking at their watches. Some were tapping the screens; some were pushing buttons.

Petra went careening onto the grass and fell flat on her front. As she pulled herself up, she could hear one of the runners shouting back at the marshals: "Did someone move the 2k marker?! I've just broken my 3 k PB! Thank you Marshal!"

This is the imaginary story of the parkrun tourist that we first met in the story about Christopher, the impatient man in the queue. This is how he came to be at Wycombe Rye trying to get a good time in a place that rhymes with Wigan.

====================================

A parkrun tourist comes to Wycombe Rye

If only the parkrun in Wigan was called Wigan parkrun thought William, as he struggled to complete his latest parkrun poem. As a lifelong man from Wigan, he'd wanted to include the name of his home parkrun in his witty poems about his travels around the country including a place that started with 'W' but unfortunately, the Wigan parkrun was call Haigh Woodland Heath parkrun, and that wasn't going to rhyme with anything.

"It's no good," he said to his wife, "I'll just have to start the poem from scratch and think of a new way of including Wigan."

William sat up all night thinking about it.

In the morning he went to his wife and asked her what she thought.

"Right here we go, let me know what you think," he said.

"OK, I'm ready, dear," she said.

William took a deep beath.

"Right, here goes: *There was an old runner from Wigan…*"

He stopped.

"And..?" said his wife.

"OK, here's the next bit, *"Who went to a parkrun*

in..."

And...?" said his wife again.

"Well, that's where I get a bit stuck; you see there are no parkruns that start with a 'W' and sound like Wigan. I'm so disappointed, I might as well give up."

"Don't worry dear, something will come to you, I'm sure of it, and don't you go around saying things like giving up, just remember you're a parkrunner and parkrunners don't give up."

"But if I want to start the poem with 'There was an old runner from Wigan, who went to a parkrun in...' I just *have* to have a place that rhymes with Wigan, and even though there are forty-four places that start with 'W', none of them rhyme with Wigan."

"Never mind dear, maybe they'll start some new events soon," she said, unhelpfully.

"I don't know, it just feels like everything is against me."

But later that evening William was watching the evening news and heard a report about a football team that had been promoted to the championship from a place that sounded like High Wick Ham. He sighed to himself as he thought how much Wick Ham sounded like Wigan. *Now that would be a good word to have in my poem* thought William. Then he saw the word written on the TV screen. His eyes widened as he looked at the word. *That doesn't look like Wick Ham*, he thought, *it looks like Why Combe be.*

Suddenly, William's eyes widened even more. He was thinking of the lists of parkruns beginning with 'W' and he could remember the strange place called Why

Combe Be Ray parkrun.

"Margee! Pack your bags, we're going to Why comb be ray, I mean Wick Ham Rye. There's a place that rhymes with Wigan! My poem is saved!"

William rushed upstairs to look at his maps. *Now, where was High Why Combe Be* he thought. He placed his finger on the map and slid down the page. *Blimey,* he thought, *it's miles away.* He needed a plan, quickly. His wife wasn't going to be happy about travelling all the way down south just to get a word that rhymed with Wigan.

He checked the interesting facts about High Wycombe; it wasn't looking promising: lots of chairs, and the first multi-screen cinema in the UK, probably because they had loads of chairs, he thought to himself, and a football team, more chairs, he thought. Yep, chairs were probably the only thing worth going to see. As he looked further, he read about a chair museum. *This is a serious chair town*, he thought to himself.

"Right pet," he said to his wife, "we're going to have a grand day out and then we'll have a look at some chairs, then maybe some more chairs, OK?

She could see that he was determined so reluctantly agreed.

They travelled down on Friday evening and stayed with a family member who had moved south many years ago so that they could take a short drive to the Wycombe Rye car park at the Lido on Saturday morning. They'd done their homework beforehand and stood in the car park queue next to a man who was very helpful in telling them about the course. He even showed them how to use the machine when it was their turn to get a ticket.

They then talked to a man called Bob who sounded like he wasn't a local and kept talking about 'Why Combe be Rye'. William wondered if the place was really called that; he wondered if it was the TV report that had pronounced it incorrectly. *That would be a disaster,* he thought, *but at least the trip to the chair museum and the six-screen cinema would make the trip worthwhile.*

William looked around and took in all the beautiful scenery, it was certainly a very nice place to have a run. There was a boating lake, and an outside swimming pool called the Lido, a children's play area, coffee shops, a waterfall, and a river. The whole area was in a valley surrounded by hills that were covered in trees. There were also a lot of Australian flags and a lot of people running around asking everyone if their name was Bob.

William started to talk to some of the regulars and found out that there were other interesting facts about the course, they kept talking about the steps and the various places around the route where people sit and watch the runners run past.

Makes sense, he thought, *might as well use the chairs around the park to watch the runners.*

He asked the locals about the chair museum and they looked at him blankly, which surprised him. He also thought it strange that they weren't very interested in the country's first multi-screen cinema at Handy Cross, preferring the Cineworld in the town centre because it was closer to Yo Sushi.

They had a word with the run director to tell them how far they'd travelled that day; they were hoping that they might get a mention as the visitors who had travelled the furthest but apparently someone had already beaten them to it. But they were delighted that everyone gave them a big cheer as they were introduced as the visitors from Wigan—which wasn't as far away as New Zealand, depending on which way you travel, apparently.

Then they were off on the run. William had a great run; he even managed to run up the steps and he also noticed how many park benches there were all around the course. He finished in 24:22 which was a really good time, especially as the numbers 2 and 22 in particular was key to the rhythm he wanted in the poem.

He stayed in the Lido Café and had a coffee with the locals before heading off to the chair museum and the multi-plex cinema. At the end of the visit to the cinema, they got in the car and travelled back to Wigan.

William had had a wonderful day and now sat at his word processor thinking about his day and composing his poem.

William's parkrun poem for the letter 'W'

==

- There was an old runner from Wigan.
- Who went to a parkrun in Wycombe.
- He checked out some chairs.
- And concessionaires
- And made sure his poem had rhythm.

- This runner he travelled with purpose.
- His wife who was with him was nervous.
- He ran up the steps.
- And knackered 'is legs.
- His wife shouted, 'Heavens preserve us!'

- When William mentioned the chairs
- He got so many blank stares.
- He went to Yo Sushi.
- Then saw a great movie.
- His wife went to Next to buy flares.

- Now William was happy at last.
- The end of his run he did pass
- The Kiwi in Black.
- Was far from the back.
- But was slipping on all the wet grass.

- When they finally entered the queue
- They were asking just what should we do.
- The token was numbered.
- But all that he wondered.
- If his time was a two or two two.

©Simon Jones 3rd October 2020